If Mic Could Fly

JOHN CAMERON

If Mice Could Fly

JOHN CAMERON

A Sparrow Book

Published by Arrow Books. An imprint of the Hutchinson Publishing Group
London Melbourne Sydney Auckland Wellington Johannesburg and agencies
throughout the world. First published by Andersen Press 1979. Sparrow edition 1980.
© John Cameron 1979. All rights reserved. Printed in Italy by Grafiche AZ, Verona.
ISBN 0 09 924500 0

If mice were like monkeys
they'd hang upside down
and bombard the cats
as they strolled on the ground.

And the cats, though hungry
and ready to drop,
would never quite catch
a mouse on the hop.